Who Hops?

HARCOURT BRACE & COMPANY
San Diego
New York
London

By
KATIE DAVIS

To my husband, Jerry,
who has helped me make my dreams come true
(kenahora ptew, ptew)

Library of Congress Cataloging-in-Publication Data
Davis, Katie I., 1959–
Who hops?/Katie Davis.
p. cm.
Summary: Lists creatures that hop, fly, slither, swim, and crawl,
as well as some others that don't.
ISBN 0-15-201839-5
[1. Animal locomotion—Fiction. 2. Animals—Fiction.] I. Title.
PZ7.D2944Wh 1998
[E]—dc21 97-37175

E G H F D

Printed in Mexico

Who hops?

Frogs hop.

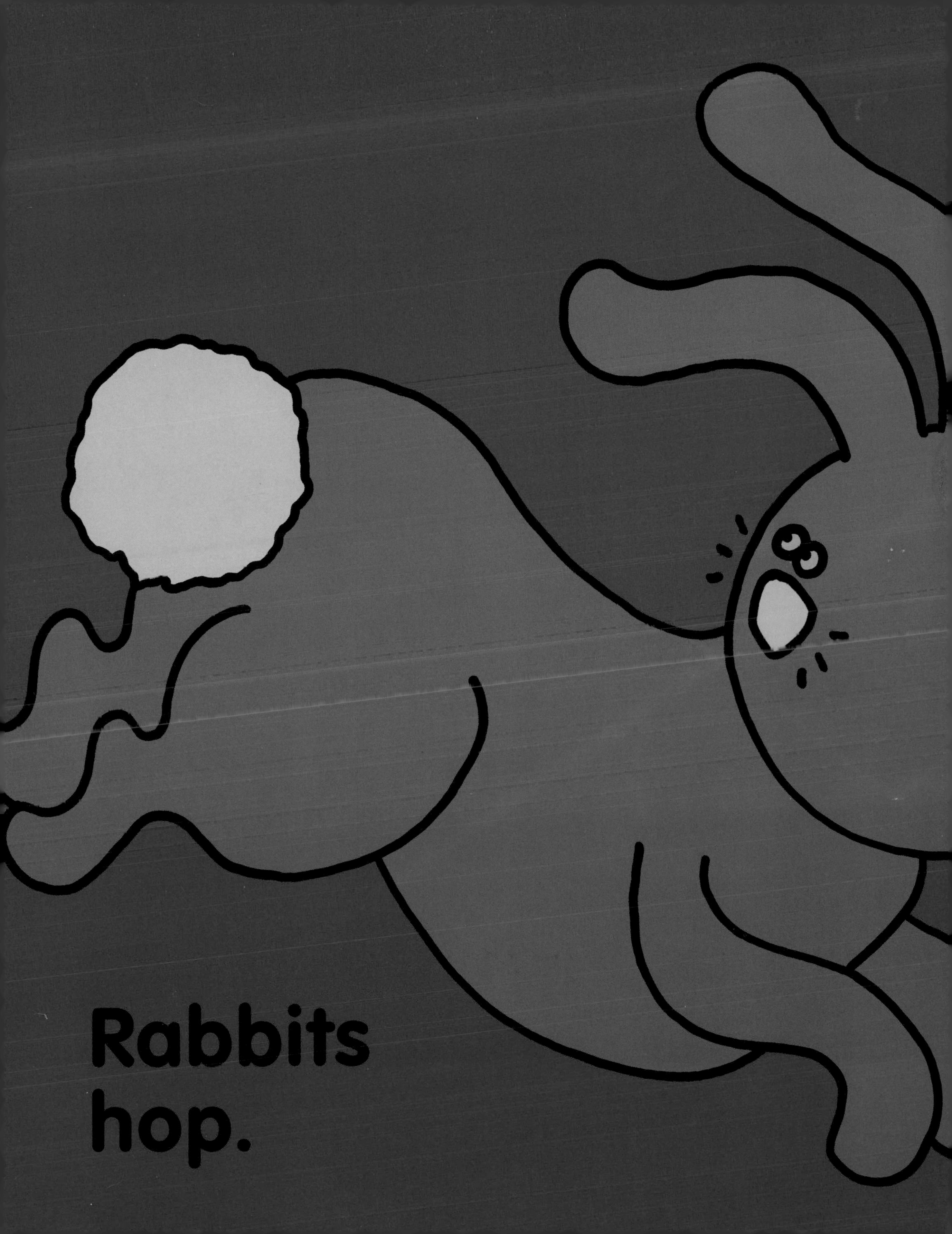

Rabbits
hop.

Kangaroos
hop.

Cows hop.

NO THEY DON'T!

It would never work.

Cows moo and give milk, but they **don't hop!**

Who flies?

Birds fly.

Bats fly.

Flies fly.

Rhinos
fly.

NO THEY DON'T!

Rhinos eat grass and take lots of baths, but they **don't fly!**

Who
slithers?

Salamanders
slither.

Snakes
slither.

Snails slither.

Elephants slither.

NO THEY DON'T!

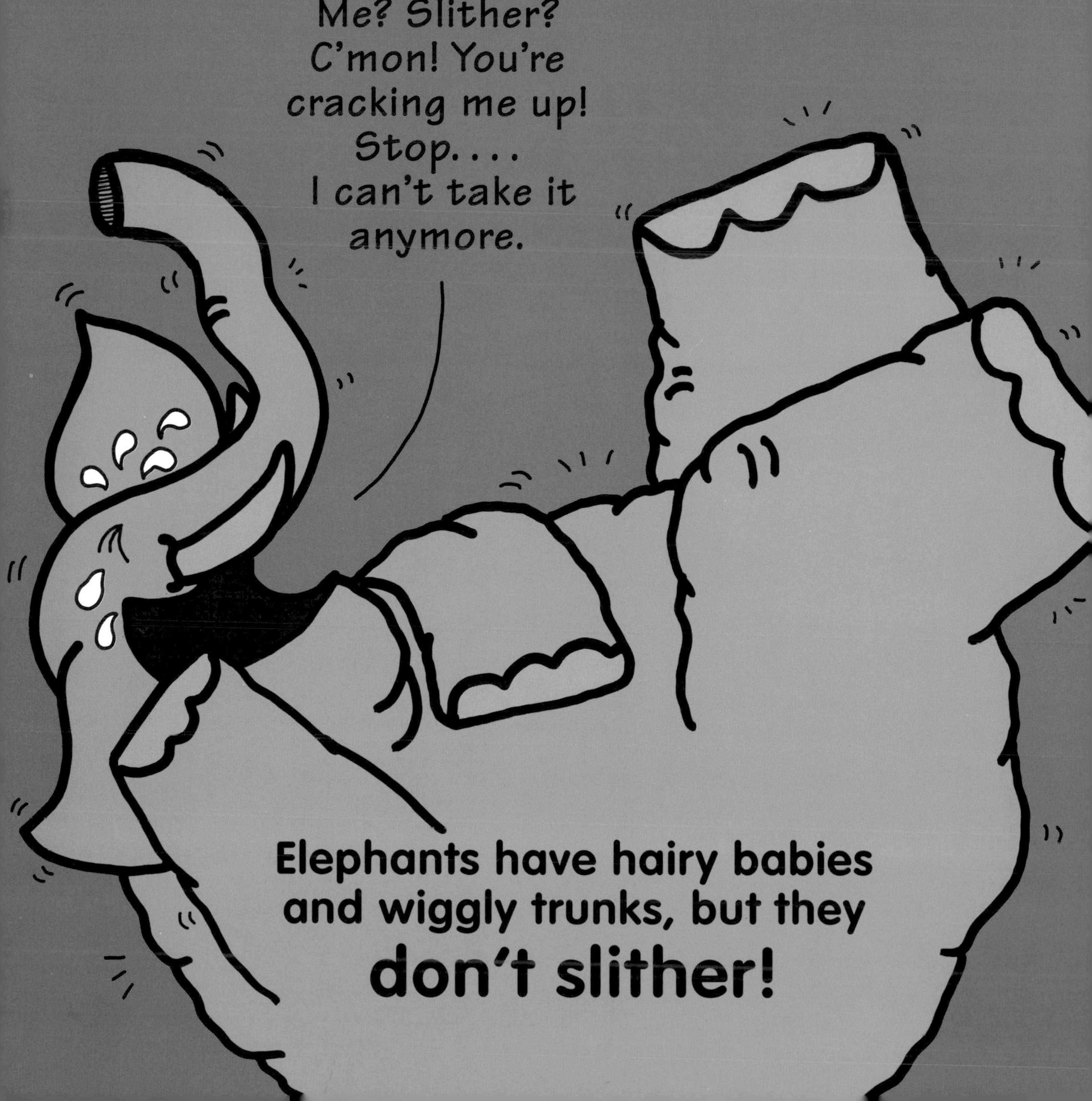

Me? Slither?
C'mon! You're
cracking me up!
Stop. . . .
I can't take it
anymore.

Elephants have hairy babies and wiggly trunks, but they **don't slither!**

Who
swims?

Goldfish swim.

Sharks swim.

Whales swim.

Anteaters swim.

NO THEY DON'T!

Anteaters eat ants and have long sticky tongues, but they **don't swim!**

I just ate, so I really shouldn't go swimming anyway.

Who crawls?

Crocodiles crawl.

Giraffes
crawl.

NO THEY DON'T!

Uh . . . not a good idea.

Giraffes eat leaves and have really tall babies, but they **don't crawl!**

Who hops
and flies and
slithers and
swims
and crawls?

You do!

I give enormous and heartfelt thanks
to my own personal superhero triumvirate:
Peggy Rathmann, my mentor and friend, who hooked me up with
Steven Malk, my genius agent, who got me to
Susan Schneider, my editor, who brought this book
to a whole other level.

Without the support and constant hounding
from my amazing critique group—
Rosi Dagit, Molly Ireland, Maria Johnson,
Ainslie Pryor, Pam Smallcomb, and Ann Stalcup—
this book would have been all wrong.

And if Benny and Ruby,
my spirited and sweet children,
hadn't played Who Hops? with me in the first place . . .
Well, you get the picture.

The illustrations in this book were done in pen-and-ink with pre-separated colors.
The display type and text type were set in Vag Rounded.
Color separations by United Graphic Pte Ltd., Singapore
Printed and bound by RRDonnelley & Sons, Reynosa, Mexico
This book was printed on totally chlorine-free Nymolla Matte Art paper.
Production supervision by Stanley Redfern and Pascha Gerlinger
Designed by Linda Lockowitz